# When I'm a Grown-up

First published in the UK in 2004 by
QED Publishing
A Quarto Group Company
London EC1V 2TT
www.qed-publishing.co.uk

Reprinted in this format in 2006

A Catalogue record for this book is available from the British Library.

ISBN 1 84538 565 9

Written by Anne Faundez
Designed by Alix Wood
Illustrated by Katherine Lucas

Creative Director Zeta Davies
Senior Editor Hannah Ray

Printed and bound in China

# When I'm a Grown-up

Anne Faundez

QED Publishing

When I'm a grown-up,
who will I be?

A bird in the air,

or a fish in the sea?

When I'm a grown-up,
what will I do?

Fly a spaceship to Mars, or work in a zoo?

When I'm a grown-up,
will I be tall?

# Huge like a hippo,

or round like a ball?

When I'm a grown-up,

what will I eat?

Pineapple pie,

or some other treat?

When I'm a grown-up,

who will live with me?

A frog or a dog?

Or a hoppity flea?

When I'm a grown-up,

what will I wear?

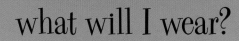

Hmm, let me see,

I really don't care!

When I'm a grown-up,
will I travel by car?

Ride on a rhino,

or swing from a star?

When I'm a grown-up,
I really don't mind
Who I will be...

as long as

I'm

ME!

# Can you remember?

Can you spot the little cakes?

What other types of food can you see?

Can you remember any of the animals that appear in the story?

What does the little girl think she

might do when she is a grown-up?

Who might
live with the
little girl
when she is
a grown-up?